ALL ABOARD THE
NUMBERS
TRAIN

Illustrated by

sean sims

OXFORD
UNIVERSITY PRESS

We're at the station. We're off to explore **numbers,** space and so much more.

All aboard!

1

One sun is shining brightly in the sky.

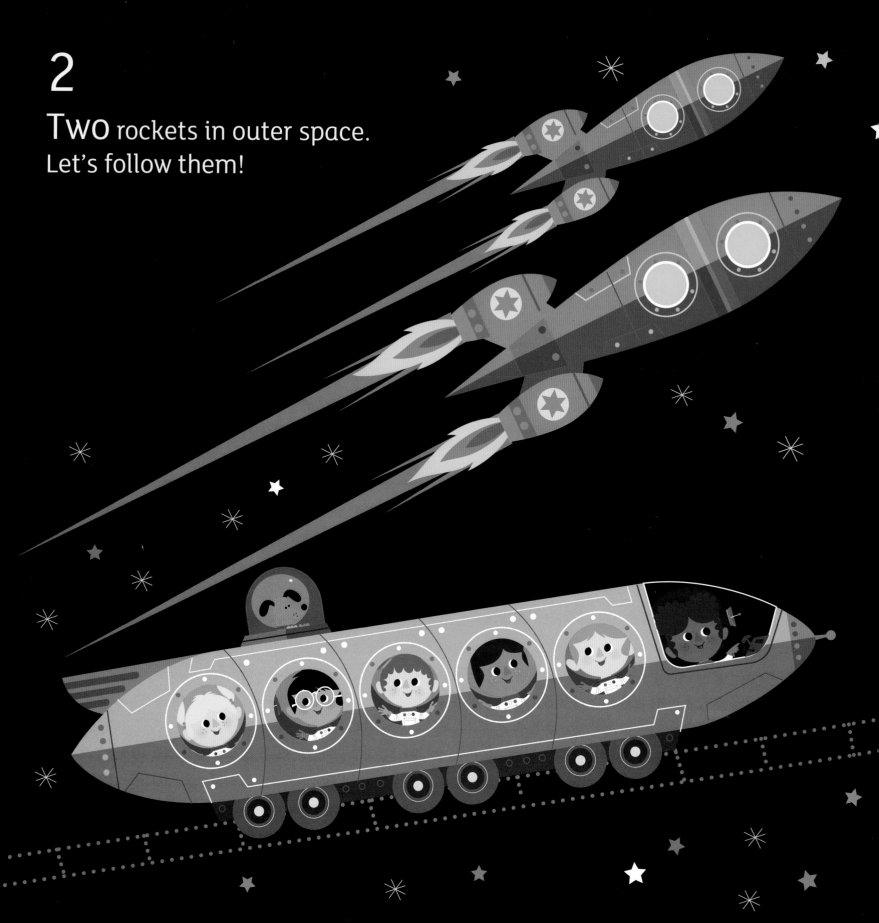

2

Two rockets in outer space.
Let's follow them!

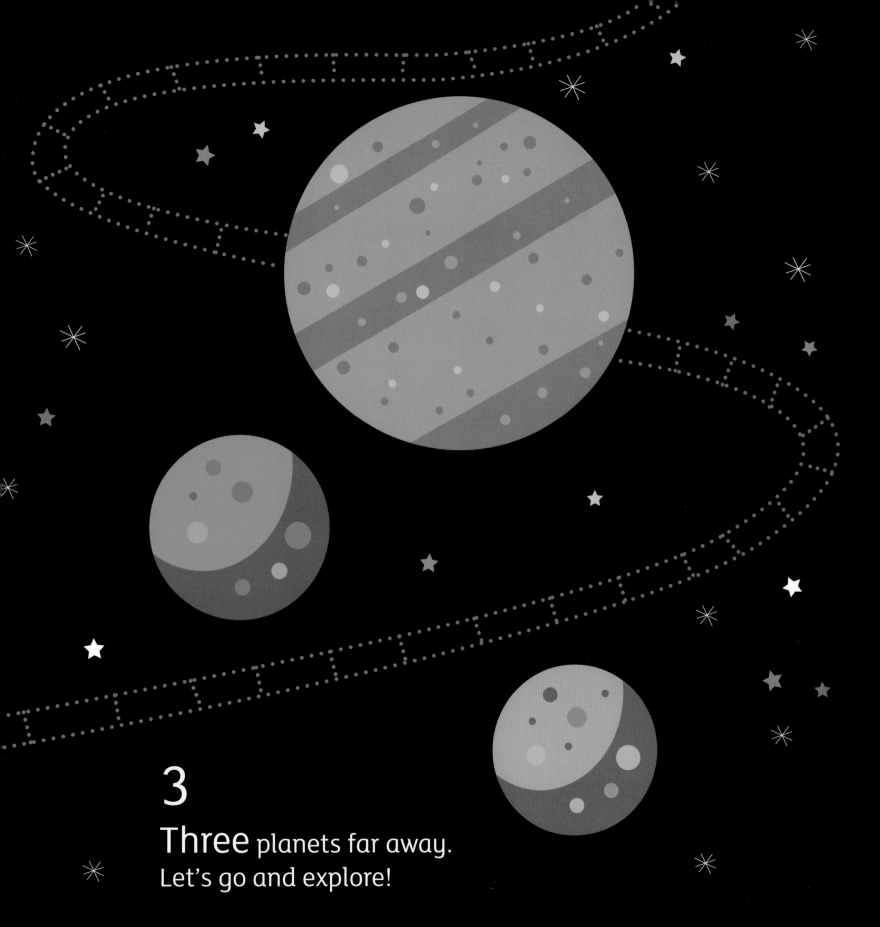

3
Three planets far away.
Let's go and explore!

4

Look! Here are **four** flags.

5
Five friendly aliens having fun.

6

Six comets, shining bright!

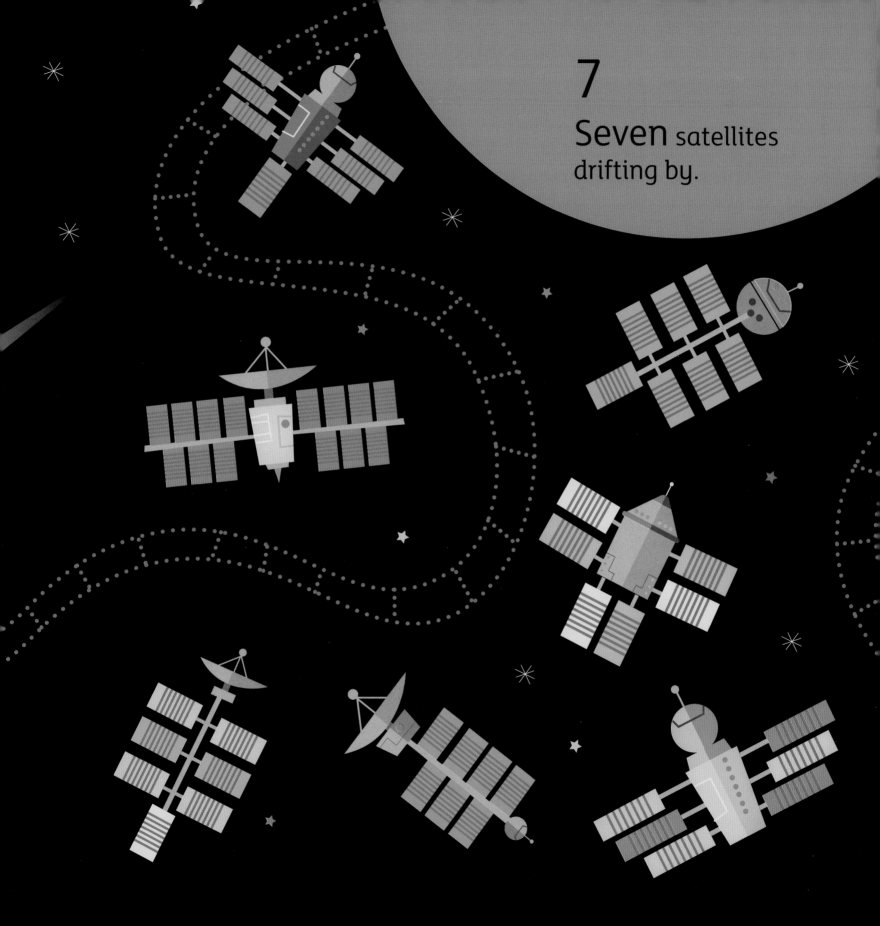

7
Seven satellites drifting by.

8
Eight rings around the green planet!

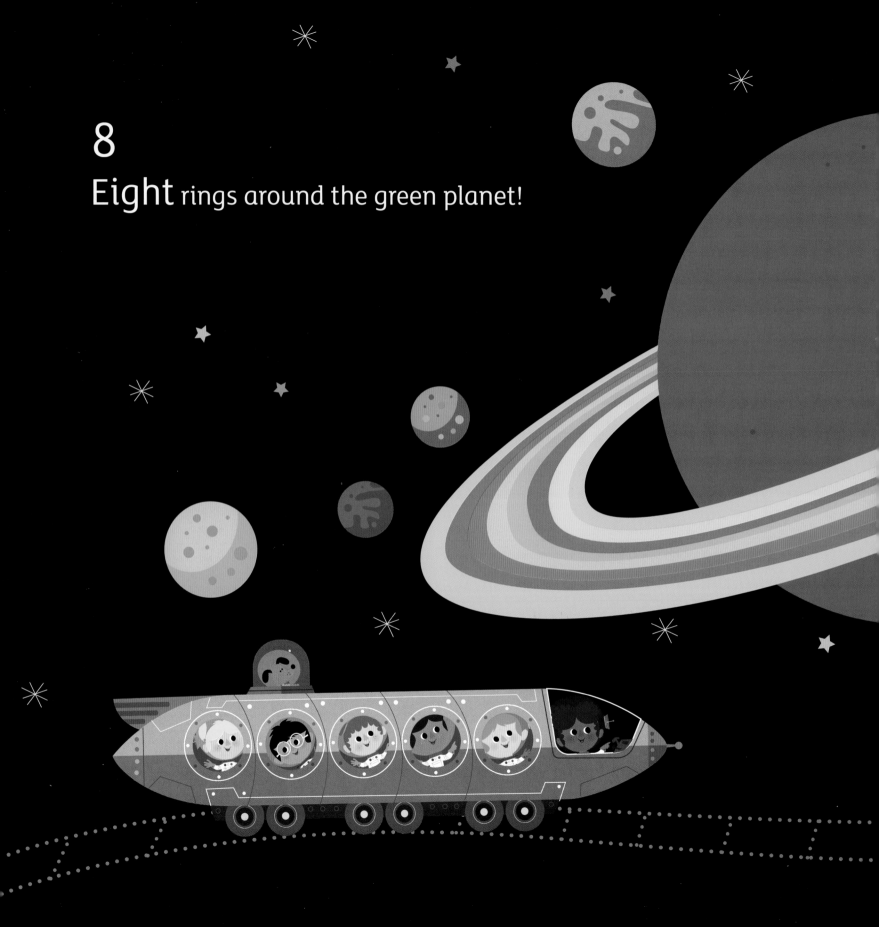

9
Can you count nine moons?

10

Ten stars shining above us.

There are lots of **numbers** inside the space train!

Can you count up from 1 to 10?

We're playing hide-and-seek with **numbers!**

Can you find numbers **1** to **10?**

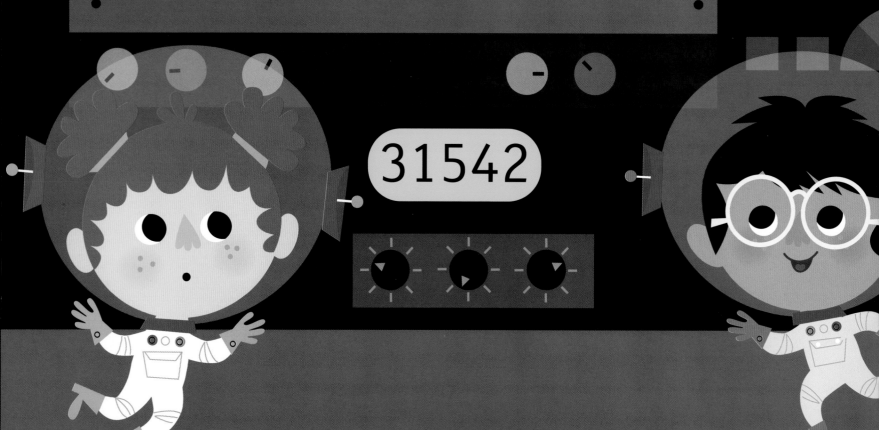

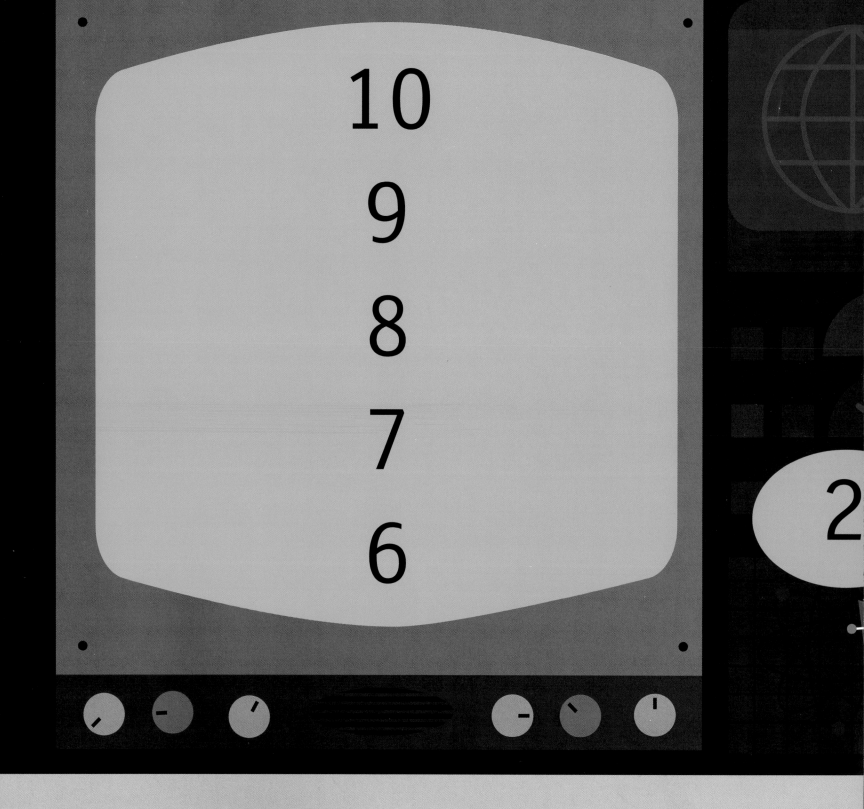

10

9

8

7

6

2

Help us to count down to our journey home!

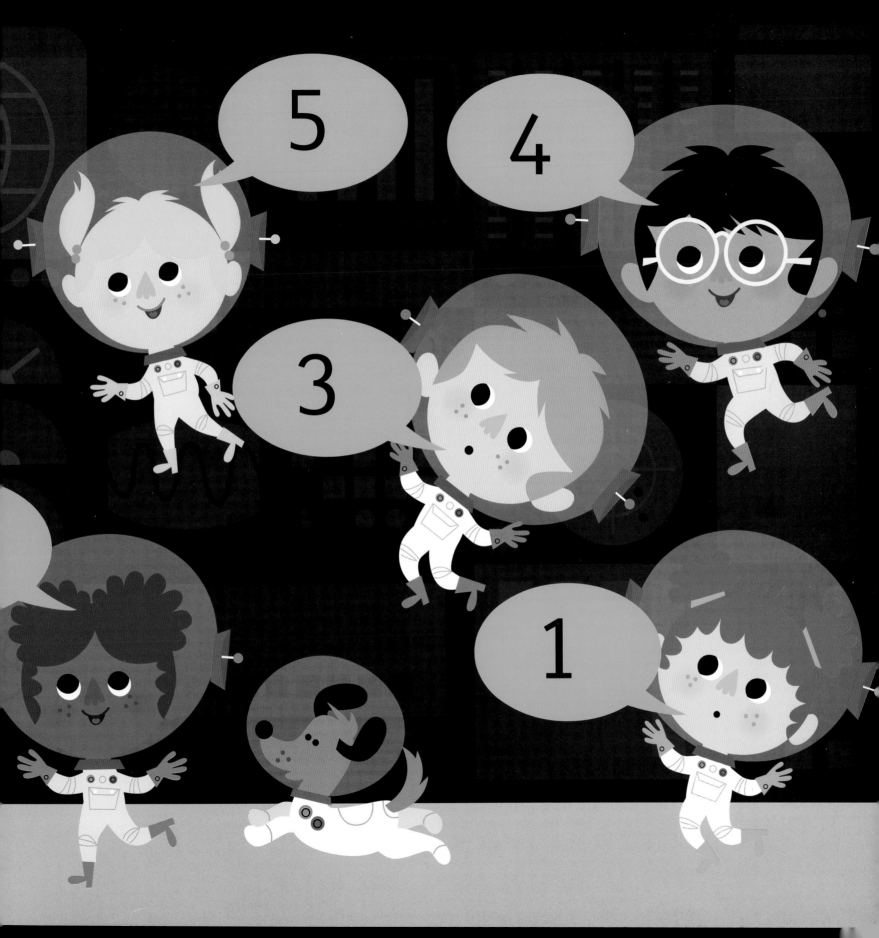

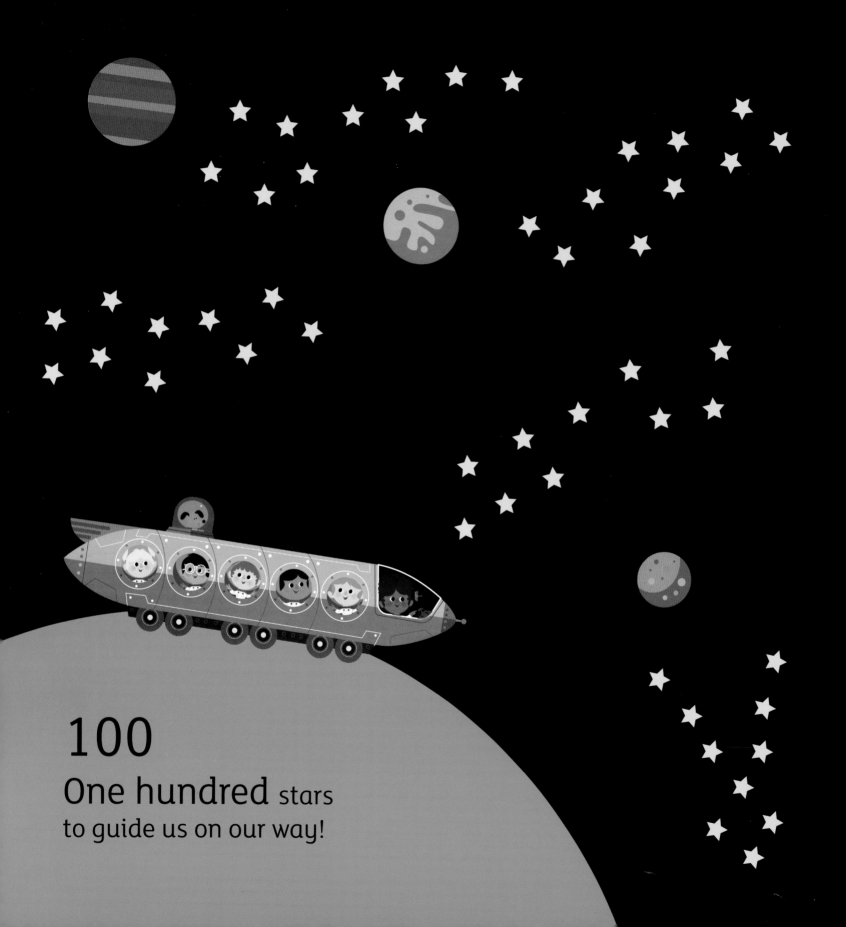

100
One hundred stars
to guide us on our way!

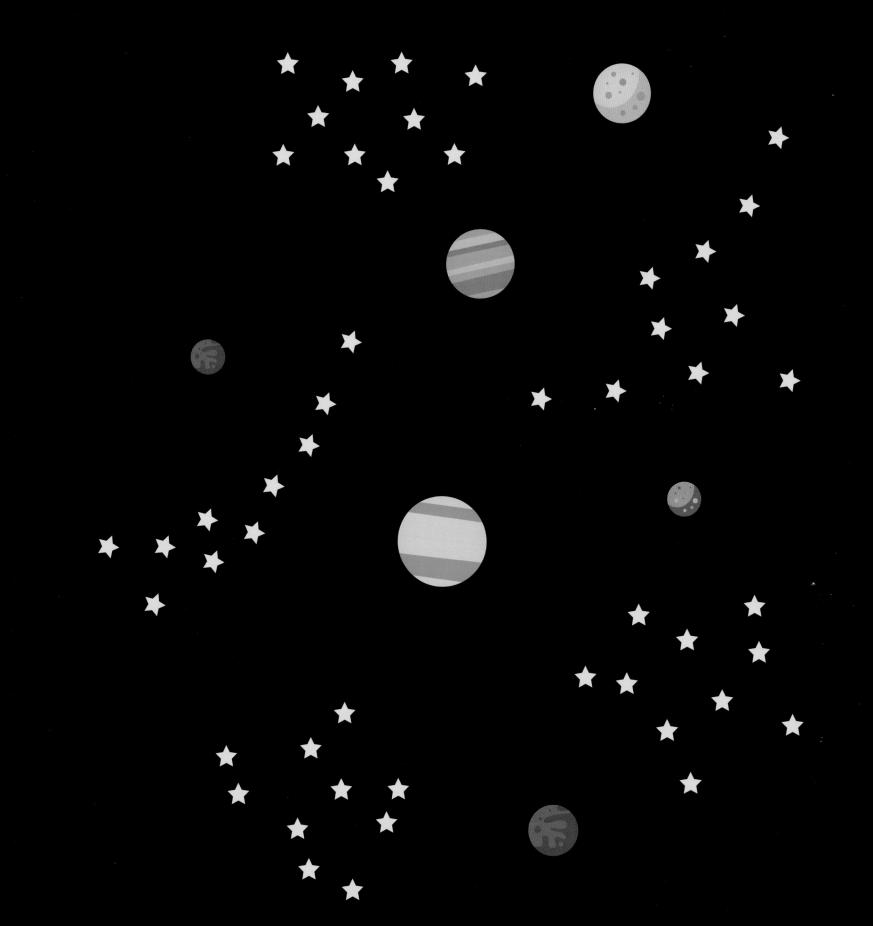

Can you remember the numbers we saw on the journey?

It's time to go home.
All aboard!

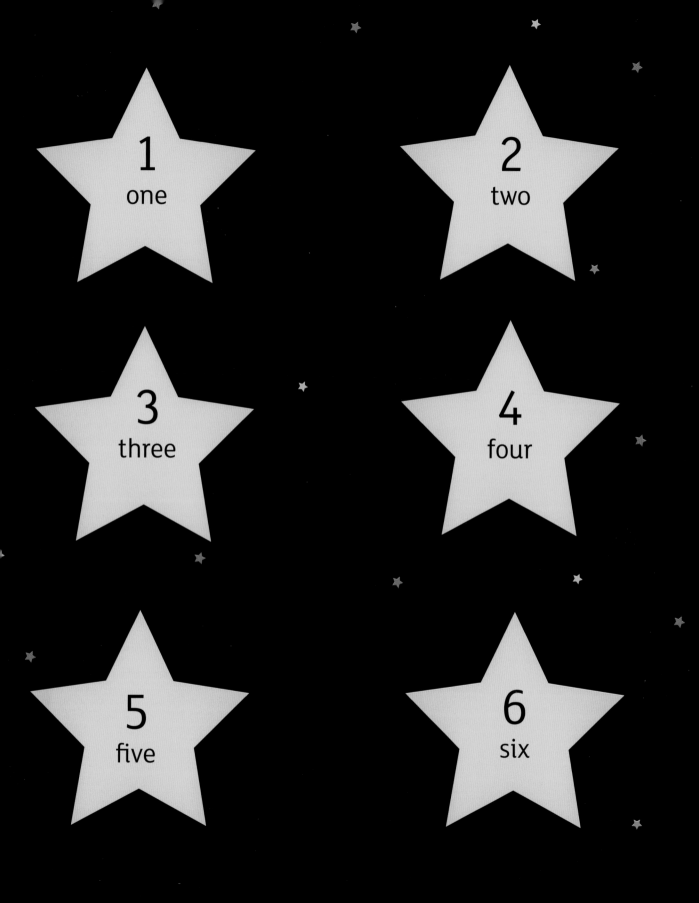

OXFORD
UNIVERSITY PRESS

Great Clarendon Street, Oxford OX2 6DP
Oxford University Press is a department of the University of Oxford.
It furthers the University's objective of excellence in research, scholarship,
and education by publishing worldwide. Oxford is a registered trade mark
of Oxford University Press in the UK and in certain other countries

British Library Cataloguing in Publication Data

Data available

ISBN: 978-0-19–277470-5

1 3 5 7 9 10 8 6 4 2

Printed in China

Paper used in the production of this book is a natural,
recyclable product made from wood grown in sustainable forests.
The manufacturing process conforms to the environmental
regulations of the country of origin.